MYRTLE

TRACEY CAMPBELL PEARSON

Farrar Straus Giroux • New York

Copyright © 2004 by Tracey Campbell Pearson
All rights reserved
Distributed in Canada by Douglas & McIntyre Ltd.
Color separations by Hong Kong Scanner Arts
Printed and bound in the United States of America
by Phoenix Color Corporation
Designed by Barbara Grzeslo
First edition, 2004
1 3 5 7 9 10 8 6 4 2

Library of Congress Cataloging-in-Publication Data
Pearson, Tracey Campbell.
    Myrtle / Tracey Campbell Pearson.— 1st ed.
        p.   cm.
    Summary: With the help of their Aunt Tizzy, Myrtle and her baby
brother learn how to deal with a mean neighbor named Frances.
    ISBN 0-374-35157-0
    [1. Self-confidence—Fiction. 2. Bullies—Fiction. 3. Aunts—
Fiction. 4. Brothers and sisters—Fiction.] I. Title.

PZ7.P323318My 2004
[E]—dc21
                                                    2003044059

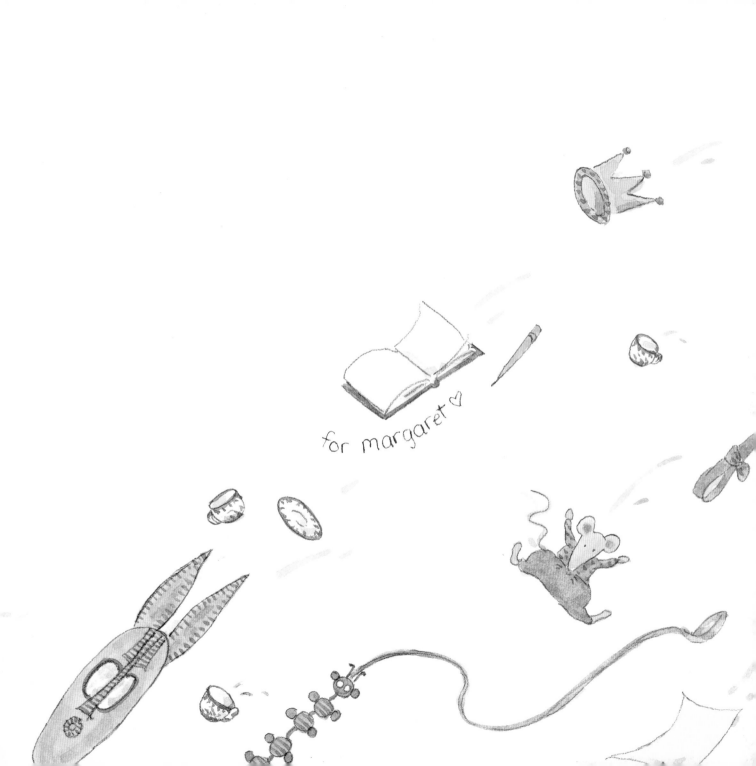

for margaret ♡

Myrtle was happy. Her mom loved her. Her dad loved her. Her baby brother loved her. She had a good life, until . . .

. . . Frances moved next door. Frances did not love Myrtle or her baby brother. Frances made mean signs, sang mean songs, and said mean things.

Frances was mean.

When Myrtle's ball rolled into Frances's yard, Frances kept it for three weeks and two days.

Myrtle only got it back because her baby brother found it. Frances
had covered it with bubble gum, and it stuck to his nose.

Frances liked to hide in the bushes and pretend she was a monster. She made the bushes shake and rumble.

Myrtle was afraid of monsters, and so was her baby brother.

One time, Frances planted rubber snakes all over Myrtle's yard.
She hissed and made them jiggle.

Myrtle did not like snakes, and neither did her baby brother.

The worst days were when Frances was quiet. Myrtle waited and waited for something terrible to happen. Sometimes it didn't . . .

. . . but usually it did.

On one of those quiet days, Myrtle decided not to go outside at all. Soon, one day turned into many.

Myrtle's parents called her favorite aunt, Tizzy, who was on a safari in Africa. "Myrtle needs you!" they cried.

Aunt Tizzy dropped her binoculars and caught the first elephant out of the jungle. Before long, she was at her niece's house.

"Where's my Myrtle?" she asked.
"In here," mumbled Myrtle from her closet.

Aunt Tizzy spent the day in the closet with her niece. They had a tea party with Myrtle's favorite toys. They giggled and played.

Aunt Tizzy had brought some African masks. They tried them all on, and they roared and they howled and they yowled.

Myrtle told her aunt about mean Frances. Aunt Tizzy told
Myrtle about the mean lions in Africa.

"Weren't you scared?" asked Myrtle.

"Sure, but I wasn't going to let a few nasty lions keep me away
from Africa," Aunt Tizzy said.

"What about when they roared mean lion roars?" whispered Myrtle.

"I told them to stop being rude, and if they continued, I simply roared back," replied Aunt Tizzy.

"Or sometimes," she added, "I would just sing and dance until they were gone."

When Myrtle came out of the closet, she felt bigger and stronger.

"We are going to have fun!" Myrtle yelled.
She grabbed her baby brother and all the toys she could carry. She
ran past her mom, dad, and Aunt Tizzy, and went outside to play.

Frances was in the bushes, singing mean songs.
"How rude!" declared Myrtle.

Myrtle and her baby brother chased each other and roared like lions. They made up their own songs: silly ones, happy ones, and noisy ones.

They were so loud, Frances could hardly hear herself sing.

Myrtle and her baby brother danced. They wiggled and squiggled and ran around the yard. They laughed so hard, her baby brother wet his pants.

Frances came out of the bushes and waited for someone to notice her.

But no one did.